Fearless

BY
RACHEL VAN DYKEN

Fearless
by Rachel Van Dyken

This is a work of fiction. Names, places, characters, and events are fictitious in every regard. Any similarities to actual events and persons, living or dead, are purely coincidental. Any trademarks, service marks, product names, or named features are assumed to be the property of their respective owners, and are used only for reference. There is no implied endorsement if any of these terms are used. Except for review purposes, the reproduction of this book in whole or part, electronically or mechanically, constitutes a copyright violation.

FEARLESS
Copyright © 2014 RACHEL VAN DYKEN
ISBN 13: 978-0991587209
ISBN: 0991587200
Cover Art designed by P.S. Cover Design

Chapter One

The human heart beats around one hundred thousand times a day. It pumps over two thousand gallons of blood through over sixty miles of blood vessels in any given twenty-four hour period. The physical greatness would be staggering enough, given those facts. But the emotional capacity? Words can't explain. Doctors can't describe why certain parts of your heart react to anger, sadness, joy, and love. Why, when you laugh, your heart laughs with you. When you cry, your heart breaks for you. But the most amazing fact of all? How easily we give our heart away even with the knowledge that in another person's hands you are the most vulnerable you will ever be. — Wes Michels

Wes

I sat in one of the pool chairs at my house. The mid-afternoon fog gathered around the Sound making it look more magical than eerie. Every time I exhaled, I could see my breath — proof that I was living.

Such an amazing experience — to know you're alive.

My muscles ached and my head felt like it was going to

explode. I was still trying to figure out if I liked living in that moment or if I wanted to stick my head in the sand and let out a little cry.

I was trying to balance wedding planning with Kiersten, drama with Gabe, and spring training with the Seahawks.

Life was quickly spinning out of control... not in a bad way, but if there was anything I'd learned in my twenty-two years of living, it was that even good things could end up being bad if you didn't put what was important first.

And Kiersten?

She was most important.

I winced as my muscles debated whether or not they were going to work or cease from functioning and let me fall on my ass.

"Wes?" Kiersten's pretty voice floated through the air. The sound of her voice was always like a balm to my soul, it reminded me of the first time my name had the honor of being formed by those beautiful lips. I could be in the worst mood — and just hearing her voice, my name and her voice mixed together, was enough to fix everything.

Moving slowly because I felt like an old man with a walker, I turned and gave her a bright smile.

"What's wrong?" She ran towards me and grabbed my hands. Her green eyes filled with tears.

"Why do you assume something's wrong, baby?"

Her lower lip quivered. "Your smile's fake."

"Aww..." I pulled her into my arms, knowing that it was going to hurt like hell when she squeezed around my midsection. "I'm just in a bit of pain, that's all."

Her eyebrows furrowed together in concern. "Your chest?"

"No." I chuckled stroking her red hair with my fingertips. "My entire body. Those workouts are rough."

"Oh." She sighed in relief, almost melting against me. "So you're fine? Your heart's fine? Everything's fine?"

"Sweetheart…" I slowly released her and looked into her deep green eyes, framed by dark lashes and flawless skin, she still took my breath away. "Are we going to have to have another one of those talks where I tell you not to freak out every time I'm doing something other than smiling?"

Her shoulders sagged. "Probably. It's just everything with Gabe and Saylor—it just reminds me of last year and… I don't know. It's too close to home, you know?"

"Yeah." I sat back on the chair, pulling her down with me until she sat in my lap. "I know." My hands instinctively dug into her red hair, my fingers twisting her silky locks. Each strand had a mind of its own as it wrapped around and slid through between two fingers, only for me to grab another piece and repeat the process. Each touch of her hair shot an obsessive need to have her—straight through me.

With a groan, she laid against my chest. "It's kind of cold out here. What were you doing anyways?"

I swallowed the panic and told myself that being nervous was ridiculous. Kiersten had seen me at my best and my worst. She could take anything.

"Remember last year? When I told you I wanted to marry you a year after I woke up from surgery?"

She tensed in my arms. "Yeah."

"So…I don't want to do that anymore."

Kiersten immediately started fidgeting with her hands. "Wes—"

"I can't wait." I stopped her from pulling completely away from me. "If I have to wait one more week I'm seriously going to lose my mind." I kissed her exposed neck and sighed against it, my body finally relaxing now that I was in her arms. "I want to get married now."

"But—"

"I lied. I wanted to be married the day you said yes."

"But—"

"I've spent my entire life being patient, Kiersten. I've

spent my life waiting. Waiting to live, waiting to die, waiting to hear good news, waiting to hear bad news. And for once, I really, really, want to be selfish and screw the whole waiting process. I want you. I want you right now. I want you in every way a man could want a woman. I want you every second of every day. I want to give you my name. I want to live with you. I want to take care of you. I want to have kids with you. I want to massage your feet after a hard day. I want to hug you when you're sad. I want to hold your hand when you're sick. I want to hold you in my arms and never let go—even waking up in the morning with our bodies intertwined, won't be enough for me. Breathing your air destroys me because I can taste you in everything—even when your lips aren't anywhere near mine—damn, I can taste them, I taste you. I want you so deeply etched in my soul that I don't know where I end and you begin. So, Kiersten, I'm going to pull the whole "I was dying and this is my dying wish card"—because every day I'm not with you. Every day that goes by when I don't get to share every single moment with you…is like waiting to die all over again. So, will you marry me? Not in another eight months— will you marry me….now?"

"How…" Kiersten's hoarse voice shook. "How in the world do you expect me to answer that?"

My chest ached deep inside like I'd held my breath for too long and my lungs were about to explode. Was she rejecting my proposal?

"I would have married you the second you asked, Wes. Had the doctors said they could only keep you alive for five minutes, I would have spent those five minutes in your arms—loving you. Time is precious—and I want to give you all of mine. So marrying you today? Even if I was in nothing but jeans and a t-shirt. Even if I was running a fever or got hit by a car…I'd do it. I love you. My heart's been yours since the minute you needed it to beat for you. So Wes…" She cupped my face and peered deep into my eyes.

With one look, she exposed everything I had ever been or would ever be. I stopped breathing.

Then her lips tipped upward in one of her gentle smiles. "My answer's yes."

"Really?" I choked and gasped for my next breath. "You mean it? Right now?"

Her eyes narrowed. "Sure. Right now."

"Oh good." I smiled, kissing her mouth once... twice, considered a third but spoke instead. "I'm so glad because that would have been super embarrassing."

Kiersten bit down on her lower lip and pulled back from me. Her gaze searched behind me then behind her.

I looked too. Nothing but swirling fog in both directions.

Those beautiful, accusing eyes returned to me, and she raised one eyebrow. "What did you do?"

"I read so many romance novels someone should seriously cut my balls off and take my man card."

"Huh?" Kiersten wrinkled her nose.

"You think I don't notice," I said, smirking. "But I see what you and your Kindle do at night." Laughing, I cupped her chin. "Why didn't you just tell me you wanted me to storm your castle? I would have totally bought a horse."

Kiersten's face flushed red.

"And, really, there were so many highlights on that one contemporary romance where the guy was a hockey player that I almost thought about trying out for the NHL."

Her blush deepened.

"But what really got me," I whispered, "was that every single one of your quotes...were about true love. About surprises and a lot of them, about being fearless."

Her eyes smiled. "You taught me that. To be fearless."

"Yeah, well." I slowly nudged her off my lap and got to my feet, bringing her with me. "I'm taking a cue from all that advice and all five hundred of those romance books and doing something really scary."

"Marrying me is scary?"

"Hell, no," I growled pulling her against my chest, kissing her head, damn just touching her shook my self-control. "But planning an impromptu wedding in front of all your friends and family without telling you? Yeah, it may have freaked me out."

"What?" Her eyes went were so wide that I was afraid she was going to pass out from the strain. "I'm sorry, impromptu wedding?"

"Surprise?" I lifted her into my arms and carried her into the house.

"But I didn't see anyone and—"

"Oh, thank God." The words came out in a rush as Lisa slumped in relief and smiled. "She said yes!" The relief was short-lived, as two seconds later Lisa was running towards us with a hairbrush in one hand and some sort of torture device in the other. "We only have like two hours."

"Two hours?" Kiersten repeated.

I set her on her feet and kissed her forehead. "See you girls at the ceremony."

"Ceremony?"

Lisa and I both nodded then shared a high five behind Kiersten's head.

"But...my aunt and uncle—"

"You think my dad would let me forget about Uncle Jobob? Geez, they're worse than two old ladies. I'm shocked your uncle kept the secret this long. Now, go get ready. I'll see you in a bit."

Reluctantly, I left Kiersten in Lisa's hands and went outside. Gabe was waiting around the corner in my SUV. When he saw me wave, he drove up and unlocked the doors. "So?"

"She said yes!"

"Thank God," he grumbled.

I paused in the middle of climbing in and frowned at

him. "Did you guys doubt me?"

"Girls are weird." Gabe lifted his hands into the air. "I think we know this by now."

"True." I smirked. "Oh, and I'm waiting."

"Bastard," Gabe mumbled under his breath then said, "Weston freaking Michels is a badass."

I cleared my throat. "And?"

"Do we really have to do this?" He groaned.

I crossed my arms.

"And, when the time comes I'm naming my firstborn after him." His head shook as he fought a smile.

We laughed the entire way to the ceremony location. Gabe said Kiersten would freak out—in a bad way. He said girls needed plans. Taking control from them—especially considering girly things like weddings—was like asking to get your balls chopped off with a rusty knife.

But he didn't know Kiersten like I did.

And that was okay.

Chapter Two

"A love so deep. A love so wide. A love so extravagant — that even death wouldn't deter me from an eternity by your side. Can you imagine that type of love, Kiersten? Can you fathom it? Well, can you?" — Wes Michels

Kiersten

Lisa tugged my hair with a brush and then set to work on braiding it into a loose crown around my head.

"How did you keep this a secret?" I gasped as she pulled a bit too hard and glared when she smiled like she'd done it on purpose.

"If I can keep my identity a secret as well as Gabe's secret life — I can surely keep a surprise wedding a secret." She grinned at me through the mirror. "Vault. I'm a vault."

"Rrrriiiight." I laughed, while she shoved a few bobby pins into the base of the braid and grabbed the hairspray.

"Hold your breath. I don't want this to fall out."

I covered my face with my hands and took a deep breath as the cold hairspray hit the base of my neck and top of my head.

"Now." Lisa set down the can. "Makeup and the dress."

I giggled—I couldn't help it. Was this really happening? Was I going to be a wife in a few hours? How the heck had Wes planned everything? It was a tie between being so nervous I wanted to puke and being so excited I couldn't actually sit still.

I hadn't told Wes—mainly because I didn't want to add to the stress, but with everything going on with Gabe, things had felt distant. I know he wanted to be there for his friend, but between practice and him making sure Gabe didn't jump out a window—I'd kind of fallen into the cracks. Though if I were being completely honest to myself it felt more like a giant chasm.

"Hey…" Lisa held out a dress. "You ready for the fairy tale?"

I gasped when she zipped open the garment bag. The color white made everything more real. The material shimmered and beckoned from the bag. The lamplight from the room gave the beading a warm glow. I was almost afraid that if I touched the dress it would disappear. "Is that for me?"

"From your future husband—he flew it in from France."

"WHAT?" I shrieked.

"Wes Michels does style good." Lisa's smile grew to epic proportions. She clapped her hands in excitement. "Then again he may have had the super awesome best friend of the bride help out a bit with measurements." Lisa giggled and thrust the dress into my arms. "Now hurry and get dressed, we don't have a ton of time."

Chapter Three

The type of love that makes you want to laugh out loud—scream a bit—run in circles—and then repeat? Yeah that's how I felt about Wes. Totally. Out. Of. Control. Giddiness.—Kiersten

Lisa

My smile felt so forced that it ached. Don't get me wrong. I was really excited for Kiersten—what type of friend would I be if I wasn't excited?

I felt like the last one. The redheaded stepchild. However, you want to look at it. Wes had Kiersten…Gabe had Saylor…

And I had…a shady past filled with the memory of a guy I'd betrayed. A guy I could have loved—but had destroyed instead.

Yeah, so much for happy memories.

"How's it look?" Kiersten emerged from the bathroom and twirled. The dress was actually an embellished bodice with a sweetheart cut, while the skirt was around seven layers of lace and intricate beading. It had a definite Spanish flair. It was something I knew Kiersten would love.

And when I'd tried to show Wes, he'd covered his eyes and pulled out his credit card and mumbled something about not wanting to see the dress before the wedding and that I should do "whatever it takes" to make the love of his life happy.

I snatched that credit card with lightning speed—no girl should say no to a Wes Michels credit card, those bad boys have no limit, which was also a perk since I'd had it shipped that very day.

"You look beautiful." I fought the tears clogging my throat as Kiersten's smile filled the room with joy. I had to look away. I needed to look away because it broke my heart that I would never have that same type of joy. That same smile. I didn't deserve it and part of me wondered if I ever really wanted it in the first place. When you want something, you fight for it, right? And I never fought. I just gave in, over and over again. I gave in to the nameless faces, the touches, the numerous advances…and then there was Taylor.

I didn't give in to him. Not the first time. Or even the second, but the third? The fourth? The fifth? Sixth? Seventh? I'd lost count. And he'd turned out to be a monster. So I'd tried to leave. But the thing about leaving someone who's a sociopath? They always find you.

For years, I'd never regretted what happened, what I did. It had to happen in order for me to survive…but watching Wes and Kiersten—it made me regret things, things I had no business regretting, because in the end I couldn't turn back time. I couldn't get my dignity back, my pride, my heart. Those had all died right along with his black soul.

Chapter Four

Plato believed that reasoning originated within the brain, but passion? Passion originated in what he called the fiery heart. Separate from all logic—fueled by blood, driven by passions. I for one, completely side with Plato, how else could I explain the way she made me feel? It went against logic. It went against life. Against death. It was transcendent. —Wes Michels

Wes

Being nervous hadn't really occurred to me—not until Gabe mentioned a text from Kiersten where she used lots of exclamations points and enough emoji to illustrate her own graphic novel. By the time we'd gotten to the location and I saw the decorations—I started freaking out. Probably not to the level that Kiersten was freaking out, but my hands were shaking and I was pretty sure that if Gabe offered me a shot of tequila I'd toss it back like water. I wasn't nervous about the marriage—I was nervous about everything before that point.

I sucked in a nervous breath as Gabe slapped my back. Either Kiersten was going to flip in a bad way, or she was going to think it was the coolest thing I could do.

Yeah, the very fact that Gabe flipped should have given me a hint. After all, the guy had just visited hell and back. To say his life had been an emotional roller coaster for the last few months would be a huge understatement. It probably didn't help that in the process I'd given him, what? Two black eyes? Hey, that's what friends do. They punch you in the face when you act like a jackass.

"It's creepy." Gabe sniffed and looked around the white room. "You know those movies where people go to heaven and everything's white?"

"Yeah?" I touched some of the flowers sitting on the table. "What about them?"

"We are freaking in that movie dude, I'm a bit worried the door's going to close on me and then a trapdoor on the floor's going to open revealing the fires of hell and a booming voice is going to come on the loud speaker and say 'MAKE YOUR CHOICE!'"

"Paging Doctor Smith," boomed a voice over the loud speaker in the ceiling

With a giant-assed start, Gabe grabbed my arm and let out a streak of curses.

I burst out laughing as I lifted his hand and dropped it. "You still worried they don't want you upstairs?"

"Cautious." Gabe pointed at me and rolled his eyes. "Just cautious."

"Everything ready?" My dad came barreling in, JoBob and Sandy in tow. Even though we were loaded, we'd had a hell of a time actually getting all the big shots at the hospital to agree to this. But honestly? Any other way and it wouldn't make sense.

I hoped Kiersten would realize that.

Saylor popped into the room and shut the door behind her. "Okay Lisa has Kiersten in the car and they're driving in this direction, so everyone?" She waved her hands into the air.

"She dancing?" I asked Gabe.

He tilted his head and squinted at her then shook his head. "Not sure."

Saylor sighed in irritation. "Just get in your places like we practiced last night."

"That was fun." Gabe smirked. "Last night."

"Can we not?" I smacked him on the shoulder. "Wedding day? Hello?"

"Sorry." He licked his lips and winked at Saylor who in turn blushed so red that I was convinced she was going to stop breathing altogether and pass out on the table. Hey, at least we were close to the hospital.

I tugged at my tie again and told myself to calm down.

But instead of calming down, my heart slammed against my chest. Funny, how I'd come so close to never having that feeling ever again. Yet there it was, slamming in perfect cadence. Announcing to the rest of my body that I was nervous, that I was excited. It's funny, we all have hearts, but do we ever truly listen to them?

Its' true, death had made me all kinds of philosophical, swear it made Gabe want to strangle me most the time.

But the question remained. How often do we hear our hearts and stop to appreciate the fact that it's been beating solid, strong, for our entire lives? God willing, your heart never stops until you finally die. It beats harder when you're sick, it beats softer when you sleep, it beats harder again when you're excited, and sometimes it physically hurts when you're in pain.

Your heart isn't just a muscle.

Though I'm sure people would disagree with me.

Your heart is everything. Why else would God ask for it first? I mean, why not ask for your mind? Your soul? Instead, God asks for our hearts. Our significant others ask for our hearts. Family...they ask for our hearts. Friends ask for our hearts.

It's not just a muscle.

I truly believed that the heart stored the essence of everything a person possessed. The human body didn't start with the brain or the legs...no...when we were conceived...the first thing doctors searched for?

The heartbeat.

When you get married...you don't just ask for your wife's hand. The first thing you search for? Her heart.

When you're sick. The doctor doesn't ask about your heart—he listens to it.

Seems to me like we've had it wrong all these years.

If you have a heart—I guarantee—there's someone out there who wants it. Who's searching for it. Who dreams about it.

"Wes?" Gabe knocked me in the shoulder. "You okay?"

"Yeah, just thinking about...things," I lied.

"Well," he said, sighing. "Pretty sure all thinking will cease the minute that girl walks through that door."

"Oh yeah?" I smirked. "Why?"

Gabe gave me a knowing grin.

Kiersten walked through the door, her eyes already pouring tears down her cheeks.

And then I looked at the bouquet she was holding.

Red roses. In the shape of a heart.

She was holding my heart.

Chapter Five

He'd given me his heart a long time ago—and now I was giving it back, not because I didn't want it. But because I wanted to share it. With him. Forever.—Kiersten

Kiersten

When Lisa drove me up to the hospital, my first thought was something had happened to Wes. Funny, how you think you can be totally over something. And then one tiny little thing happens and immediately you're back to that place. I wondered if PTSD was like that.

You live your life every day, going through the motions, and then BOOM! Something suddenly happens to throw you off kilter and the only thing you want to do is go sit in a corner and rock back and forth.

When she parked and didn't start crying or saying that we were there because the man I loved was dying—again. I lost it.

Too close to home.

I wanted to leave.

Actually, I wanted to smack Wes and then I wanted to leave. How dare he scare me like that!

"Hey!" Lisa grabbed my hand. "You need to do this."

"I don't want to." I knew I sounded like a whiny child, and Wes had probably gone to a lot of trouble to use the little chapel at the hospital. But I didn't...I couldn't. My throat felt thick as I tried to swallow.

I hadn't had a panic attack in a really long time.

But being back in that hospital, even in the parking garage, was doing some serious damage to my nervous system.

I didn't want to stay and fight. I wanted to run away. I wanted to run in the opposite direction of the memories of Wes lying in that hospital bed. Of the look on his face when he said goodbye. My breath hitched in my chest as my stomach clenched with fear.

Of the tears in his eyes when he wasn't sure if it was going to be for a few hours—or forever.

I sniffled.

Lisa handed me a tissue and started slowly rubbing my back. "Talk to me, Kiersten."

"It feels like yesterday," I whispered. "I'm terrified that when I walk in that door, he's going to be back in that hospital bed, or worse, something's going to happen. I just—I know it's not logical but I don't feel very logical right now."

"It's your wedding day." Lisa shrugged. "Who says you have to be logical?"

I smiled through my tears.

"If it makes you feel better." She continued rubbing my back, totally something my mom would have done. I loved that girl, I would seriously die for Lisa, and I think she knew that. "I haven't gone back either."

"To the hospital?"

"No." She stopped rubbing for a minute. "Home. I haven't faced my demons at all. It doesn't make it easier you know."

"Are you sure?" My lips trembled as a few tears ran over them.

"Positive." Lisa handed me another tissue. "Just because you avoid something, doesn't make it disappear. I think we'd like to imagine life works that way. But I'm sure if I went back home...everything would be just how I left it and I'd be bombarded with the same memories, the same regrets, the giant never really dies Kiersten, not until you throw the damn rock."

"Nice metaphor. Hanging out with Wes too much I see."

Lisa snorted. "Swear his philosophies just rub off on everyone in his path."

I twisted the tissue between my hands. "Your giants...what are they?"

A troubled expression clouded her eyes, and Lisa sighed. "They're ugly."

"Like the ones you see in movies?"

"Yeah, Kiersten, like the ones with giant warts and giant feet and..." She shuddered. "There's a very good reason I came up to Seattle." Her smile was forced. "Look at it this way. At least you have someone willing to fight alongside you. And he's waiting inside."

"What about you? Where's your partner?"

Lisa was silent for a minute, then she reached for the handle to open the car door. "He no longer exists."

She didn't offer any more information, but the momentary distraction of her story was enough to get me out of the car and walking towards the elevator.

The smell of medicine burned my nostrils.

We rode the elevator up to the main floor, but when the doors should have opened it just kept going.

"Um?" I pointed at the buttons. "Did we miss our floor?"

"Nope." Lisa looked straight ahead, a smile curving at her lips.

When the doors opened—it was to floor where they had performed Wes's surgery. I'd remember it anywhere. The nurses' station was decorated with so many flowers it was almost impossible to see their heads as they waved at me from the table.

A banner hung across the hallway. "Wes and Kiersten." There were hearts on either side of our names.

Music started playing from somewhere. My legs had officially stopped working—so much that Lisa had to push me. I walked numbly towards the nurses' station, as each of them stood directly in my path, holding a rose.

A song started to play over the loudspeaker or it sounded like it, the music was slow, eerie, gentle as it softly played in cadence with my footsteps as I neared the nurses.

Every nurse held out a single rose, and I accepted them from each in turn as I passed, still holding onto my sense of numbness. Lisa took the roses from me and placed them in a type of bouquet. I couldn't make out the shape.

"We're so proud of you guys." One of the nurses who had been in the operating room pulled me in for a hug and kissed me on the cheek.

Okay, so Wes was seriously trying to make it so that I had no makeup by the time I saw him.

As I collected the last rose—I think around ten nurses total had each handed me one of the red flowers—I found myself at the end of the line.

The doctor that had performed the surgery stood waiting.

He was the one who had spent countless hours making sure the love of my life survived.

I hadn't been back to the hospital.

I'd thanked him.

But I hadn't *really* thanked him.

Without thinking, I threw myself against his chest and wound my arms around his neck. He went completely still for a minute and then returned my hug.

"Thank you..." I whispered, warm tears streaming down my cheeks. "Thank you for saving his life."

The doctor gently pried me away and handed me five red roses and whispered, "I wish I could take credit." His eyes blurred with tears. "But some hearts—don't need help to keep beating."

He stepped out of the way, and Lisa handed me my bouquet. It was all the roses, arranged together in the shape of a heart.

Wes's heart.

In the palm of my hands. Where it had been all along.

We walked up to the room where Wes's surgery had taken place.

When the door opened, Wes was staring straight at me. His smile wide—he looked gorgeous in his black suit.

He held out his hands and whispered, "Where we thought we may see the end—"

"—we write 'The Beginning'." I finished.

Chapter Six

I wonder how many times we think our lives are over—how many instances we scream at the top of our lungs when things aren't going our way...how often, do you think, the reason for things not going our way is because there's a bigger plan we can't see yet? A bigger destiny we could have never possibly imagined for ourselves? Maybe...we'd be a lot happier, if we were silent more. —Wes Michels

Wes

"Lamb?" I tilted her chin towards me then brushed a soft kiss across her lips. Her mouth trembled.

"Yes?" Kiersten grinned through a tear-stained face. "Big bad wolf?"

"No blowing houses down," I teased. "I'd rather build one with you. How's that for changing my ways?"

Kiersten threw her arms around me and squeezed my neck.

A few throats cleared.

"Right." I stepped away. "So we should probably get married now."

Her face was tear-stained—and gorgeous. She nodded and let me lead her farther into the surgical room where our families were standing. Everyone was standing near the wall—everyone but Uncle Jobob, who was standing by himself holding a bible in hand.

Kiersten gave me a confused look.

I just shrugged my shoulders and continued walking. We stopped once we reached JoBob.

"Your parents..." Uncle JoBob started, his voice loud, and clear as it echoed throughout the room. "...would be so proud of you." His eyes shimmered with tears.

I gripped Kiersten's hand. My heart performed a little flip at the fact that I was actually going to be marrying her in a few minutes. And that dress? It was gorgeous. Exactly what Lisa had described. Simple in its form. It was head to toe silk, with a lace overlay. It didn't take away form Kiersten's beauty—nothing ever could—but merely added to it. She wore her hair piled around her head, wisps of red fluttering around her face and loose strands trailing down her back.

She was like ice cream. Like a chocolate cake. Like the perfect desert.

"We are gathered here," Uncle Jobob said.

Kiersten's mouth fell open. "You're marrying us?"

"—sweetheart, don't interrupt the man marrying us," I whispered with a gentle laugh.

"Rude," Gabe said from behind me. "Seems wolf failed to teach lamb manners."

"Go back in your shell, turtle," Lisa murmured.

I burst out laughing while Uncle Jobob gave us a stern look then glanced at my dad who was also trying to hide his amusement.

"As I was saying..." Uncle Jobob glared at Kiersten and continued. "We're gathered here to celebrate the life of Wes and Kiersten and their desire to join together as one." His hands trembled as he held them out in front of him. "Love is often measured unfairly. People throw the word around so flippantly that society rarely gets a true glimpse of what it means to love something—to love some*one* so much that it's the basis for your entire existence. To love someone so much that you'd be willing to trade places—even in death. Well, I can't imagine a stronger type of love than that of sacrifice. So your marriage, Wes and Kiersten, is not only a celebration of a new beginning, but of the sacrificial love you share with each other."

JoBob dabbed his face with a tissue and went on, "Gabe, the rings."

Gabe stepped around me and handed the four rings to JoBob.

"Wes, wanted to do things a little different." He winked at Kiersten. "So, son, I'll just let you take it from here with your vows."

He handed me the three rings that would belong to Kiersten.

Looking into her green eyes was so distracting it was hard to remember what I was going to say. My entire body shook with the emotion of the moment. I would never get this moment again. I wanted to do it right—the first time.

"The first ring," I murmured, sliding the platinum diamond encrusted band up her finger, "represents your past. Your parents, your life in Bickelton, your first year at college, and finally the hospital room. There are ten diamonds in this band, representing every item you put on your bucket list. These diamonds are a reminder of how far you've come." I cleared my throat and slipped the next band on her finger. This one was a three-carat solitaire. "This band is the present. This moment. Right now. Every time you look down at this ring, I want you to remember the way you looked on this day. The way you made me feel. And since you can't see yourself and since you can't read my mind…" Tears filled Kiersten's eyes as I gripped her hand tighter. "You look like an angel.

Like the first person a dying man would see when he was granted access into heaven. Your skin is glowing so much that it almost hurts to look at you, the way your hair falls against that same glowing skin is so distracting that I don't know where to look first. Your eyes are really clear, because you've been crying, and your lips are a bit swollen from licking them too much, something you do when you get nervous." I placed her hand over my heart. "And right now I feel like I can do anything. My heart feels strong for you, my desire isn't just to marry you and let this be our moment, Kiersten. I want to marry you and create a million moments every single day. Which is why…" I slipped on the next ring. It matched the first one. "This ring has ten stones. I figure that we should just keep it an even number when it comes to lists. Just because the last list was finished, doesn't mean we can't create a new one. On this list, I see kids, careers, our first house, possibly our first big fight where you make me sleep on the couch. This last ring is our future, Kiersten. We complete our lists together, we complete our life together. This is what we have to look forward to. Blank pages just waiting to be filled with our story. And the cool part? We don't know what's going to happen, but I can make a promise to you right now. Your hand's going to be in mine the entire time. Kiersten, I swear to never let you go. Through sickness, through health, through happy times, through sad times. I'm yours."

JoBob handed my band to Kiersten, she took it and looked down than looked back up at me. "I don't—I didn't prepare anything, there was no time and—"

"Words were never needed between us, Kiersten," I said softly. "You know that. I can hear your heart. That's all that matters." I rested my hand against her chest and smiled as she slowly took my other hand. She squinted at the writing on the band.

"It says my name?"

"Yeah."

"With a heart?"

"Just in case I need you to keep me going and you aren't around." I smiled. "I'll just look down and remember, you're with me. Forever. Always."

"I am." Kiersten slipped the ring on my finger and then placed her hand over mine.

"By the power vested in me from Randy Michels and that handy little online tutorial..." JoBob winked. "I now pronounce you Mr. and Mrs. Wes Michels. Son, you kiss that bride of yours."

Our mouths collided, meeting in the middle. Kind of how our relationship was, the perfect give and take.

My fingers dug into Kiersten's hair as I pulled her closer to me.

She wrapped her arms around my neck.

I couldn't stop kissing her.

Time paused for me—in that moment it was like the sun had stopped shining, the earth had stopped its movement on its axis.

Out of the corner of my eye, I saw the table.

The very table that I had lain on months ago.

I remembered the cold metal of the instruments they hooked me up to, the slow steady beat of my heart on the monitor.

Kiersten stepped back from me, turning our kiss into a hug. Everyone clapped but my eyes were still on the table.

Angela had held my hand as I fell asleep.

Funny, because she held my hand during the surgery. I'd felt it. I had felt her warm palm, the imprint of the ring against my skin.

I could have lost my faith in that moment, instead I chose to believe that I couldn't control the outcome and just trusted in the hand that was holding mine. Sometimes that's all we have. A hand.

But most the time.

If we're being completely honest with ourselves.

It's all we really need.

My eyes flickered to the door. I could have sworn in that moment, I saw a nurse with blonde hair smiling, and then, as if I'd just imagined it, the figure disappeared.

My dad moved to stand in front of me, and pulled me in for a hug. "Your mom would have been so proud."

I smiled and stared at the door. "Yeah. I know.

Chapter Seven

Our steps define us—whether they take us in the direction towards what we want the most—or away from what we love. Our entire lives are based on steps and stages. Funny thing, feet. You control them. –Kiersten Michels

Lisa

Wes and Kiersten made their way through the crowded hallway, hugging doctors, nurses, patients. It was like watching a really sad Hallmark commercial or something. Not that it was sad, more of a happy sad. My smile was frozen a bit on my face—actually it was starting to hurt...bad. I wondered how actors did it. How did they act happy when they were torn up inside? I would have been the worst actress on the planet.

Even as a model I hadn't been that great, thus the reason for nobody really recognizing me when I moved up to Seattle. I'd dyed my hair and grown out of my lankiness into more of an athletic build. To a model—that was a curse. Muscle tone! Oh no! But for me? It was as if I had finally been given a gift from above. Finally, I was able to look in the mirror and see someone other than that girl from so many years ago.

"Hey!" Gabe wrapped his arm around my shoulders. "You look...off."

"Ah..." I turned my head to meet his gaze and gave him a friendly pat on the chest. "Music to every girl's ears."

Gabe's gaze narrowed. "What happened?"

The guy looked less haunted these days, as if he'd finally caught a break and was able to live a normal existence where he wasn't always worrying about keeping his secret. That's just what he didn't need, more drama. I slung out from underneath his arm and penetrating gaze and shrugged. "I'm pregnant."

"WHAT!" he roared.

I burst out laughing. Wow! I'd so needed that. Veins I didn't even know existed popped up on Gabe's forehead and neck. I took pity on him and winked "I'm kidding."

"Hilarious." He coughed a few times and then leaned over as though he had to catch his breath. "Never again Lisa, or swear I'm going to lock you up. Okay?"

"Um, okay?" I rubbed his back and winked at Saylor who was watching our exchange in amusement from her discussion with her mom over at the nurses' station.

"So..." Gabe stood to his full height. "What's really bothering you?"

"Nothing," I lied, pasting a smile on my face. Everything was bothering me. Every damn thing. But it was stupid. I mean compared to everyone else's drama, my little insecurity and inability to forget my shady past really wasn't that big of a deal.

"Look..." Gabe lowered his voice and continued. "I know it's hard, with Wes and Kiersten getting married, and me and Saylor...if you need to talk it's totally fine and—"

"Holy crap, Gabe!" I smacked at him and stepped away. "Clearly I'm not acting like myself if you feel the need to go all therapist on my ass! Geez, I get that enough with Kiersten and Wes. Do you even realize how hard it is hanging out with those two constantly bugging me?"

Gabe narrowed his eyes. "Um yeah? I was their target for a whole year, remember?"

"It's not that." I crossed my arms. "I think I'm just exhausted from school and stuff. Maybe I need a vacation."

"So go on vacation." He made it sound so easy so simple.

"By myself?" I whispered and rolled my eyes. "Sounds like loads of fun."

"Take the girls."

"Honeymoon."

"Are you just going to reject every awesome idea I have?" Gabe countered.

"No." I scratched my head. "You know what, yeah, a vacation. Maybe I'll do that. Um, I'll catch up with you guys later."

I strolled away from him as fast as my black heels would take me. Each step helped me breathe a little easier. Maybe that was it. Their happiness was suffocating me or something.

Hands shaking, I stabbed the elevator button and quickly got in.

The elevator made it all the way to the second floor then started shaking. The lights flickered and the little alarm went off.

Trying not to panic, I counted to three and then pressed the main lobby button again.

Nothing.

A voice came over the intercom. "Sorry ma'am, minor electrical issue. We'll have you out in no time."

Shit!

The last time I had been stuck in an elevator, things had not ended well. Honest moment, things hadn't started well either, but still...

Was this how God was repaying me? Karma was a bitch.

I went over to the corner and closed my eyes. I tried to hum a song, then I checked my cell phone. Of course no service. Naturally. Where the hell was that nerdy little man in those cell phone commercials saying "Can you hear me now?" NO man with black glasses and way too many friends, I can't freaking hear you and if I don't get out of this tiny little shoebox of death I'm going to freak the EF OUT! Swear it felt like the walls of my throat were closing in right along with the walls of the elevator. I punched the wall above the control panel, right because punching things always made them work. I'd karate chop its ass and take the chance of slicing my hand up if I knew it would work.

Struggling for my next breath, I smacked the elevator door around five times, making my hand sting like crazy. When the elevator still didn't budge, I slowly sank to my knees and let out a little sob.

It wasn't the elevator.

It wasn't even the wedding or Gabe.

It was me.

I was the problem. I was *always* the problem…

He had peppermint-flavored gum—I could still taste it. I coughed a bit and then gagged—crap I was going to puke.

The darkness was the worse—not being able to really see him that well since the electricity was out—but knowing he was touching me, feeling his hands on my hips as they slid across my skin.

Shivering, I continued holding my knees and squeezed my eyes shut as his laughter penetrated into my soul.

I hated him…

Hated him so much it made me want to scream—how do you even hate someone who doesn't exist anymore?

Yet there I was in a stupid elevator, rocking back and forth like a lunatic.

"Ma'am, just a few more minutes." Someone said over the speaker.

I didn't trust myself to speak.

Minutes later, the elevator jolted to the lobby floor and the doors slid open. I got up off my butt and bolted for the main doors to the hospital. I was a bit impressed with my ability to run in high heels. Had Gabe seen me, he would have yelled that I was going to break my neck. Hah! No death for me. Because the last thing I wanted was to join...*him* in the afterlife.

Shivering, I started the car and made my way back towards campus. It was September, classes were starting that week, and I still hadn't gotten my schedule together.

I parked by the student center and marched towards the doors, my high heels clicking against the pavement. I could do this. I was confident. I wasn't Mel anymore. I was Lisa, a college student, free from my past, free from the memories of him, free from everything that held me back—that kept me in LA when it was slowly killing me inside.

Not really paying attention to anything except for walking and breathing at the same time, considering the whole elevator incident was hell on my frazzled nerves, I jerked open the door to the center and was nearly knocked on my ass by someone pushing the same door I was pulling.

I stumbled backwards. "Hey watch where you're—"

"Mel?"

My entire body froze—instantly paralyzed with fear. It was one of those moments you experience when you're a little kid and you hear a freaky noise down the hall. You're so terrified you just—pause. All you can feel is your heart beating against your chest, and your own ragged breathing. Ginger and caramel colored hair, grey eyes—oh, God the eyes. Muscles lining every part of his body. Hulking shoulders. Hands, huge hands. My body shook at the memory of hands just like that, touching me, pushing me, hands I'd trusted—hands I'd at one time in my life—loved. The guy in front of me reached out, just as instinct kicked in.

I turned on those tall heels and ran like hell back towards

my car. It took me four tries to get the key in the ignition. I sped out of the parking lot and turned in the direction of the dorms.

My body was still shaking by the time I pulled up in front of my place. I couldn't call Kiersten. She'd just gotten married. Wes would kill me.

Gabe was already married so...did that mean he was fair game?

He'd kill me if I didn't call him.

I chewed my lower lip and then finally, with trembling hands, dialed Gabe's number.

"Hey, where'd you go?"

"He's here." My voice quivered. "He's here, Gabe."

"Who?"

"T-Taylor!"

"Sweetheart..." Gabe sighed. "He's dead, remember?"

"No!" I hit the steering wheel. I wasn't crazy. I knew what I'd seen—*who* I'd seen. I had seen the guy who ruined my life—who ended his own. I saw him! "I'm not crazy."

Swearing, Gabe whispered into the phone, "Where are you?"

"The dorms." I looked behind me just to make sure he hadn't followed. Right, because it was totally possible for a human to chase a car two miles and actually arrive at the same time. Then again, ghosts could do just about anything right?

"I'll be right there."

"I'm going crazy." Saying it out loud made it scarier. "Aren't I?"

Gabe didn't say anything for a bit and then sighed heavily into the phone. "You're not going crazy. You're just really stressed, okay Lisa?"

I nodded even though he couldn't see me.

"Is it possible you saw someone who looked kind of like Taylor?" he asked gently.

"I guess, but he knew my name! My *real* name!"

"Lisa, I hate to break it to you but half the known universe knows your name right now—especially after the story about me went viral for months. It's going to happen."

I breathed a little easier. "So maybe it was just…me being…stressed?"

"Lisa, you've been burning the candle at both ends. Planning everything for the wedding, keeping Kiersten in the dark. Do me a favor?"

I rolled my eyes. "What?"

"Relax. Go to your room, make yourself some hot chocolate, take a shower, and read a magazine. Just unplug for a bit. Classes don't start for another day. Just take time for yourself. You deserve it. We've all been through hell this last year."

My eyes searched the parking lot again.

No Taylor.

So I was either stressed, or I was losing it. I chose to believe it was stress, going crazy so wasn't in my life plan!

"Thanks, Gabe." I slowly unlocked my door and started getting out of the car. "I'm sorry for interrupting you guys."

"Lisa…" Gabe's voice was soft. "You're not an interruption. I'd die for you. You know that, right?"

"Yeah." My lower lip trembled. "I do." I cracked a smile. "Best cousin ever."

"Ha-ha," he teased. "Very funny."

"I'll just…go see about that bath now."

"Do it. I want to hear all about your relaxing evening later on okay?"

"Deal."

"Bye, cousin."

"Bye, turtle."

We hung up. I slowly walked towards the dorms and shook my head. Yeah, I was just stressed. Either that or I was going to give that little kid in *Sixth Sense* a run for his money because I totally saw dead people.

Real cool.

With a practiced smile, I slid my keycard over the pad and went into the building. Inside was some hot chocolate with my name on it.

Chapter Eight

When you hear bad news it's like a literal punch to the stomach—no seriously, your body will create a physical response to your emotional trauma. When you're heartbroken—you're chest will actually hurt. Doctors believe that it's possible to die from heartache, kind of makes you wonder the opposite right? Take for example a heart that's so full, so alive, so vibrant, so—overjoyed, that it decides to skip a beat, pump a little bit longer, a little bit harder, a little bit...more than the way it was created to be. I think that's my heart—No I know that's my heart. When I see Kiersten. My heart is the opposite of broken— it's full.—Wes Michels

Wes

"So…" I brought Kiersten's fingertips to my lips and gave them a little kiss, but it wasn't enough, so I tasted…each and every one.

Funny how a person can actually taste a certain way, to me, she tasted like heaven, which is kind of ironic since I'm pretty sure last year this time I should have been charging towards those pearly gates—or would have been had I not met her. She was my savior, miracle or not. The very fact that she'd said yes to my proposal? And that we were married?

Yeah, forget surviving cancer.

I just married the most beautiful woman God ever created — period.

"So?" Kiersten giggled. "Were you gonna finish that thought or just daydream a bit? What's going on in Wes Michels Land, hmm?" She winked and then withdrew her hand from mine, placing it in her lap.

We'd just gotten into the car and already I was nervous about the rest of the night — not because I didn't know what I was doing but because I'd built up so much anticipation for this very day that, now she had said yes? And she was my wife? Well all those emotions came charging down leaving me totally wiped.

It was hell trying to hide my yawn.

Kiersten ran her fingers through my hair as I pulled onto the freeway. "You look tired."

"I look awesome," I corrected. "And...satisfied."

"Oh." Kiersten shrugged. "So I guess that means you don't need this?"

I merged into the carpool lane and glanced in her direction. Dangling. White. Lace. Bra. Holy mother of —

"Wes!" Kiersten laughed. "Stay in your lane!"

I screeched to the middle lane then almost slammed on my brakes just because my body was clearly losing all ability to function. It was like adrenaline surged through all the wrong parts forcing me to slam on the brakes while simultaneously wanting to reach over and pull Kiersten into my lap and just — I don't know, I honestly couldn't get past the white, the lace. Shit, why was I repeating myself? IN MY HEAD.

"Uhhh..." Throat dry I tried clearing it, but it only made things worse.

"Water?" Kiersten handed me a bottled water. Thank

God.

I took a sip just as she hiked up her dress and showed me her garter.

The water sprayed out of my mouth onto the steering wheel of my Porsche Cayenne.

I hacked, I coughed, I hacked again, then wiped my mouth with the back of my hand all the while Kiersten laughed her ass off and continued flashing parts of her body.

Cursing, I took the next exit.

"Where are we going?" Kiersten's laughter died down as she glanced out the window at the Sound. "A parking lot? We're pulling up into a parking lot?"

Words weren't really my thing at that moment. I was more of an action guy anyway, right? I nodded, screeched into a parking spot, threw off my seatbelt, and launched my body across the console, pulling Kiersten towards me with such force that I probably would have bruised her chin had my lips landed anywhere else but on hers.

Ah, that taste.

With a groan, I moved my left hand down her thigh. Coming into contact with that one garter was hell on my imagination.

Because, naturally there were two.

Because she had two legs.

Holy—there were two.

Garters.

I kissed her harder.

"What else?" I panted, grabbing at the back of her head with my right hand, tugging her hair, pulling at whatever I could to get her closer. "What else do you have?"

Kiersten pulled back, her face appearing innocent. Right. Nothing innocent about what was going through my mind because of that little stunt. Didn't help that her face was flushed, her color peaked. Damn, what I wouldn't' do to be able to kiss her senseless right about now. "What do you mean?"

"Any more surprises?"

She grinned. "Why? Afraid you can't handle it?"

"Sweetheart," I moaned. "My heart can only handle you in small doses—anymore and it may damn well burst."

Kiersten's expression turned serious as she removed her hands from my neck where they were wrapped so tightly I'd probably have bruises in the morning. She shrugged just before she reached for her zipper. As her fingertips touched the metal she locked eyes with me. I licked my lips, my chest rising and falling with so much anticipation I was having trouble breathing. The sound of the zipper lowering had me leaning towards her.

Kiersten drew it down farther and farther with agonizing slowness, my imagination went crazy with possibilities.

"Sorry to disappoint you," she said seductively. "But I don't have any other surprises..." Her smile turned deadly. "Just me."

The dress fell.

We were in a parking lot.

And the top of her dress just—fell open.

And she was right.

She had nothing else—because she was naked.

I don't know how long I stayed that way—in such shock that my mouth wouldn't close, my heart hammered, my mind raced.

And then, she pulled her dress back up and sat back against the seat. "So, we should probably get going...unless you'd rather hang out in the parking lot. But no way am I telling my kids that story."

"Huh?" Clearly, I was having trouble catching up—part of my brain was still functioning on the level of garters, white lace, and nakedness. To be fair, I was a guy so yeah, that was my only excuse. Well that and I loved her—more than life itself.

"Wedding night in a parking lot downtown Seattle?" Kiersten's nose scrunched up..."Not romantic, now drive." She hit the dash and leaned back.

"HOW ARE YOU ACTING NORMAL?" My voice was hoarse—damn, was I yelling?

Kiersten burst out laughing.

"Damn Lisa."

"Oh, this wasn't Lisa's idea, nor was it her gift."

"What?" With shaking hands, I buckled my seatbelt. Where the hell was north? South? East? Were we supposed to go east?

"Gabe." Kiersten released a dreamy sigh.

"I'll kill him with my bare hands if he said the word naked to you. Swear."

"No." With twinkling eyes she whispered, "But he did say something about how there's no point wearing lingerie—when it doesn't even stay on for three seconds."

"And the garters?"

"Oh these?" She flashed me more leg while I accidently hit my thumb on the steering wheel trying to start the car again.

"Yeah." I didn't look away. What was the point in trying when I didn't have to?

"All. Me." Kiersten leaned over the console and braced my face with her hands. "I got them a while ago with one intention and one intention only."

"Yeah?" I focused on her green eyes. "What's that?"

"To stop Wes Michels' heart." She laid a warm palm against my cheek and whispered, "Did it work?"

"Kiersten..." I brushed a kiss across her lips. "You stopped my heart the day I met you—re-started it—and gave it a new rhythm. You are my heart. So yeah, I think it worked."

Chapter Nine

Skin. Just touching his skin, feeling his warmth, incredible how much it made me want to weep. Like, actually fall down on the ground and sob my eyes out because by touching his skin, by feeling that warmth, I knew he was alive and by knowing he was alive, I realized...being married to him? It was totally real. Funny, how sometimes we need to keep touching things so we know they're real—even better? That I'd spend the rest of my life touching him, touching Wes Michels. And every touch would remind me, that blood flowed through his veins, that his heart beat strong, that it beat in perfect cadence with mine. —Kiersten

Kiersten

Wes was still staring at me. I fought between wanting to actually stay in that parking lot and letting him maul me—and driving off so we could be alone.

"I love you," I whispered. "Just in case you weren't aware."

"I'm aware," Wes said quickly, his blue eyes widening a bit as if trying to take in more of what was in front of him.

"With every word that comes out of your mouth. Damn Kiersten, if all you did was say nonsense all freaking day. If you talked gibberish but still looked at me the way you're looking at me now—I'd know. I'd know without a shadow of a doubt that you were mine."

I nodded, unable to really speak. Wes had a way of doing that to me, one-upping me or really just putting into words what I wasn't capable of speaking. It was as if he knew my soul and was able to explain the depth of my heart without actually asking me in the first place what I was trying to communicate.

"But—" Wes closed his eyes for a brief moment and buckled his seat belt. "The parking lot, probably not the best place to attack you and that—" He licked his lips and hit the steering wheel. "Yeah…I'm undone."

"What?" I laughed nervously. "What do you mean?"

"Undone." He stared straight ahead. "When a person reaches the end of their rope only to find out they're only half way through their journey but lack the nutrition and energy to get there. You've stripped me of all my defenses, I'm like a camel without water—"

"Do camels need that much water to—"

"The point—" Wes chuckled, glancing in my direction. "—is I have nothing left. All I want is you. My entire focus is on you. My soul desires yours, my heart beats with yours, my life won't continue in the direction its supposed to—without your hand to lead the way. So as much as I want to sit here and stare at you like a complete lunatic who's lost his mind…" He sighed and pulled out of the parking lot. "I have a surprise for you. Alone. Away from watchful eyes. Alone. God, Kiersten, you have no idea how much I want to get you alone."

Wes pulled back onto the freeway and then took the next exit. He didn't look at me, just kept talking. "I need you alone so I can spend every second, every minute, every damn hour, worshipping your body." He took the second downtown exit towards Pikes Place. "I could spend years just staring at your hair, let alone your eyes, your lips, you drive me to distraction. Like I said you undo me, I don't feel complete when I look at you but like a total mess of emotions, like I have no control over anything except for the fact that I know with a fierce determination that you were made for me and I was made for you." He stopped the car at the first stop light then drove down the hill and parked in a random spot in front of the Sound. He turned the car off, unbuckled his seatbelt and turned towards me. "I can't explain. I wish I could. I wish there were words I could use, really big words, pretty words, words that would make you swoon and cry all at once. But all I have is this…" He sighed, tears welling in his eyes. "I am yours. And you are mine."

My eyes blurred as Wes gripped my left hand in his and pressed an open-mouthed kiss to my palm.

The thing about Wes? It was impossible to respond to most of the things that came out of that guy's mouth. It would be like blowing out a candle. His words seeped into my soul and stayed there.

He stayed there.

I closed my eyes, gripping his hand in mine.

I was his.

He was mine.

Squeezing his hand, I opened my eyes and let out a little breath. Together, we'd stormed the gates of hell, and returned unscathed. Whatever life had for us, whether it be illness or any other giant—we'd go into battle together. Because he wasn't just my husband, but my friend, my partner, my lover.

My everything.

"We're here." Wes unlocked the doors.

I looked around. "Downtown? Are we staying in a hotel down here?" That would be really fun. I mean, I kind of expected Wes to do something different. Not that staying at a hotel downtown wasn't cool, but he did just marry me in the same room he almost died in so, yeah…maybe a bit of a letdown.

"Just wait." Wes winked. "Oh, and this is for you."

He handed me a black scarf.

"Er, you shouldn't have?" I took it from his hands and dangled it between us.

Chuckling, he swiped it from my hands and quickly tied it around my head. "Can you see me?"

"You have a serious issue with blindfolding people," I grumbled, crossing my arms over my chest.

He laughed and then tugged the blindfold tighter.

"Are you waving in front of me right now?" I asked.

"You tell me," he whispered.

"Yes?"

"Lucky guess." He laughed. "Now sit still while I grab our bags and attempt to walk you across the busy street without getting hit by a car." The car door slammed and when mine opened seconds later, the smell of rain tickled my nose. "Pretty sure my six-year-old self would give me a high five if he could see me now," Wes boasted.

"Because you were able to blindfold your wife and park within the lines?"

"Hilarious." Wes pulled me to my feet. "And no, because I get to play real-life Frogger with my wife!"

I sighed, shoulders slumping. "Let me guess, I'm the damn frog."

"High five."

I lifted my hand and received a slap from Wes and more laughter. I tried to stay serious I mean he did just call me a frog on our wedding night, but his laugh was infectious.

"You love me." Wes kissed the top of my head. "Admit it."

"Only if you admit that you have a problem with blindfolds."

"You really think you're in a position to complain?" Wes's hands moved from my face and landed on my shoulders, and then slowly, his fingertips grazed my breasts as his hands moved down to my hips.

I shuddered.

"Thought so," he whispered. "Now, hold my hand, while I romance you."

"In a parking lot. Playing Frogger. Blindfolded." I counted the three things off on my fingers. "Seems like you have a lot to make up for."

"I brought Red Bull." Wes wrapped his arm around me. "Believe me when I say, you'll be my entire focus...not just for the next few hours, but the rest of our lives."

We started walking. No idea what direction, but we went slowly. "Almost makes up for the Frogger comment."

"Believe me, in about fifteen minutes, you won't even remember your middle name let alone the fact that I compared you to a video game."

The sound of traffic blared in my ears. We stopped, and then walked across the street. I only knew it was a street because I could look down and see the asphalt.

The road slowly turned into a sidewalk, and then, we were indoors. I just had no idea where.

"Wait here."

Wes left me on a soft couch. The fabric felt like velvet beneath my fingertips. Were we in a hotel? Or a restaurant? It smelled good. Shrugging, I sat and waited. Waited while Wes Michels went about doing what he does best—shock and awe.

I was happy to wait—until I heard an ambulance in the distance, and then all of a sudden—I was back where I was last year. In the hospital. Waiting for Wes to either live—or die.

Chapter Ten

I started crying for no reason. It was lame really but suddenly my brain went to that possibility—what if. What if things had turned out differently. What if Wes hadn't made it. And I wasn't sitting in a lobby or restaurant waiting for his smiling face. I hated that I was torturing myself but there it was, the fear. Trying to seep into my very soul. Because a world without Wes was like a world without the sun. Pointless and dead. My world would be dead.—Kiersten

Wes

Checking in took a lot longer than I thought it would. I felt bad for leaving Kiersten sitting in the lobby, but I wanted it to be a surprise. I'd planned everything perfectly, not that it saved me from having to fill out so much damn paperwork that I seriously almost broke the pen in half.

"Enjoy," the receptionist said with a smile.

"We will." I offered a warm smile in return and walked back to where I'd left Kiersten.

Even wearing a blindfold she looked beautiful. But

something was wrong, her shoulders were hunched, and she was holding herself like she needed comforting, like the world was crumbling around her and she was powerless to stop it.

"Sweetheart?" I knelt down in front of her and grabbed her hands. "Are you alright?"

"Y-yes," she whispered. "I think so." A solitary tear slid down her cheek.

Panicking, I rose to my feet and then sat next to her, pulling her in my arms. "Are you hurt? What happened? Did something happen? Talk to me."

"My heart." She let out a pathetic sigh. "Sometimes even though I know in my heart that you're alive and you're here, I just—I go back to that place. I go back to the nightmares, the moments when I realized I might lose you forever. It sucks, and it's unfair and it's totally ruining what I'm sure is going to be an amazing wedding night, but it's just...Wes, it's terrifying, crippling." She shuddered and then reached for her blindfold with shaking hands. I stopped her before she could take it off.

"Kiersten, do you trust me?"

"Y-yes."

"Then leave the blindfold on, sweetheart." Her hands were like icicles. I brought them to my lips and kissed each fingertip. "I want you to be able to focus on my voice—nothing else. Not the fear, not the anticipation of where we are, but every word coming out of my mouth." I released a heavy sigh and leaned in so that my lips were grazing her ear. "Kiersten, the worst has happened. I should have died. I didn't. I'm right here. Next to you. Holding you. When your mind tries to take you to that place—you need to fight it. The battle is in your head. The minute you start giving power to those thoughts you've already lost. Fear wins. Don't let fear win, Kiersten. Love—our love—it can't flourish where fear is present. Do you get what I'm saying?" I pulled back a bit to watch the reaction on her face.

More tears, and then a muffled, "No."

Chuckling, I squeezed her harder. "This could be my last night on this earth. I could choose to be afraid and hole up in a hotel room or I could live. Remember you always have a choice. Don't let your mind cripple what your heart already knows to be true." I gripped her hand and placed it over my heart. "And Kiersten even if it was my last night. I would do nothing different. Absolutely nothing. Because I'm with you. My other half, my soul mate."

Kiersten nodded. I couldn't tell if she was better or if she was still upset. I thought the tears were gone, but I was still concerned. With a sigh, I helped her to her feet and led her down the hall. She adjusted her blindfold with still-shaking hands.

"S-sorry," she mumbled once we'd been walking in silence for a bit. "I didn't mean to get all…emotional."

"Yeah." I rubbed her back. "But I did call you a frog so I guess we're kind of even."

"True." She giggled. Ah, there was the laugh I was waiting for. The one that made me want to slay every damn dragon in her way and conquer the world over and over again.

All for one giggle.

One laugh.

Yeah, I was done for.

We were in the best suite they had at The Market Inn downtown. It was a beautiful boutique hotel, but I chose it for a specific purpose, one I hoped would make Kiersten cry happy tears…

"Are we at a hotel?" She asked once I pushed open the door and helped her make her way inside.

"Yup."

"So is that the surprise?"

"Nope."

"Okay…"

"Keep walking straight." I lined her up so she wouldn't knock anything over. "I'm going to open the sliding glass door really quick and then I'll take off your blindfold. Alright?"

Kiersten nodded, her smile making me feel like it was Christmas morning and I'd just gotten her a puppy.

She shivered as I led her outside. The moist air had a bite to it, so I took off my suit jacket and wrapped it around her small frame.

"The ocean." Kiersten lifted her nose into the air and sniffed. "We're right on the Sound?"

"Yeah." I watched her like a crazed fool, watched while her smile grew at the idea that we were near the water. "So, my surprise?"

Hands on hips, she shouldn't have even known where to stare, but there she was, blindfold in place, expecting something like a piece of jewelry or maybe even something like a boat ride.

"Have a seat." I gently sat her on the wooden lounge chair and took off her blindfold. Her green eyes were still a bit wet with tears. I leaned down and kissed each cheek and whispered. "Surprise."

Her eyebrows shot together in confusion. "You're my surprise?"

"Would that be enough?" I tilted my head.

"Yeah." She reached for me. "Every day of my life that would be enough, more than enough."

I backed away from her so that I could focus. It seemed every time her skin came into contact with mine, my knees felt like they were about ready to buckle and my brain screamed for me to do something about the way she made me feel.

"Your wedding present." I smiled and pointed across Elliot Bay.

"You bought me...a boat?" Kiersten guessed her eyes darting across the bay, obviously trying to figure out where I was pointing.

"Hmm, you're getting warmer." I kept pointing in the direction of the piece of land across the way. "Hey, maybe these will help." I handed her some binoculars and winked.

With a teasing scowl, she snatched them out of my hand.

I didn't look at where she was looking—no, I watched her. Because I knew I'd recognize the minute she discovered her little surprise.

With a gasp, Kiersten jerked back and then look through the binoculars again, then looked at me, then back through the lenses.

"Y-you…" She covered her mouth with her hands.

"I?" Grinning, I pulled her into my arms. "Yes?"

"You." Her lower lip trembled. "You bought us a house."

"I did."

"The house I saw last time we went to that bed and breakfast across the bay—the house with the red door."

"Yup."

"The house that wasn't even for sale when we first saw it."

I shrugged sheepishly. Yeah, it had been hell to get the people to move out, but when I offered them twice the market rate and told them my story, I was almost afraid they were going to try to give it to me for free. Had they not been an elderly couple that vacationed in Florida half the year I wouldn't have even pushed it.

"Look again," I whispered. "This time see if you can't focus on the large bay window in the front."

Kiersten, shakily lifted the binoculars back up to her face—but this time when she saw the rest of the surprise, she dropped them and fell into my arms sobbing.

Because above the window I'd had a metal sign made for all to see.

It read simply…*The Beginning*.

Chapter Eleven

Emotions are a funny thing. They drive us to either make good or bad choices, they can either make our day or ruin it. Emotions for the most part cant' be trusted because a lot of times, they help us justify our own bad behavior. They allow us to stay mad at someone, to take offense, to keep forgiveness at bay because we've been hurt or are still hurting. That's why, I can honestly say, when I look at Kiersten? It's not my emotions speaking—but my heart. Because the heart is pure in its pursuit—whereas your emotions can cause you to stumble. Why in the hell would I want to stumble in the race towards owning every part of her soul?—Wes

Wes

When Kiersten didn't stop crying, I panicked. Had I gone too far? I knew she was still sensitive about everything that had happened, but I wanted to prove to her that the house we bought...it *was* our new beginning. The fresh start, the one we had dreamed about, the one we'd stayed up late in the hospital to talk about.

I rubbed her back, trying to calm her down, but if

anything, my touch made it worse. She didn't stop trembling.

And then without a word, she shot out of the chair and freaking attacked me—not in the sense that the tiny girl beat me with her fist and it tickled like she had a feather in her hands. Hell, no. She launched herself into my arms, wrapped her legs around my waist, and kissed me so hard on the mouth that I stumbled backwards, nearly colliding with the sliding glass door and giving myself a concussion.

With a grunt, I gripped her body in my hands and lifted her higher so I wouldn't' drop her then returned her kiss.

With. Every. Damn. Ounce. Of strength I had.

Kiersten's response was to drop the jacket I'd lovingly placed on her shoulders and claw at my shirt.

Denying her would be like willingly shooting myself in the foot.

I freed up one of my hands and opened the sliding glass door then stepped through and shut it behind us. Kiersten opened her mouth, sucking on my tongue, making my knees shake a bit and blood roar in my veins. Where the hell were the bedrooms? I saw a living room, I saw no bed, I saw a hallway, okay hallways were good, right? Because they led to rooms?

"Holy shit." I bit off when Kiersten's nails dug into my back. Was my shirt off? How? How was that physically possible? I'd been holding her and then…I looked around, pieces of my shirt lay around the floor. I broke off our kiss. "Tell me the truth—were you Wonder Woman in another life?"

Kiersten's answer?

Her clear green eyes narrowed as she wrapped her arms tighter around my neck and tugged my ear with her teeth.

"Yup," I said hoarsely. "We'll get you spandex later."

Gently, I let her slide down my body and set her feet on the floor. Staring into her eyes, I smiled, and then I grabbed her hand and made a run for it. I was the romantic guy, the one who took things slow, the one who wanted to savor every moment with the girl I loved.

But right then? In that moment? I was a man possessed with such an obsessive need to claim what was mine—that I ran.

I freaking ran.

Like I was going for a Superbowl Ring and I dragged Kiersten behind me.

I pushed the first door open.

Bathroom. I groaned. "You've *gotta* be kidding me."

Was I sweating?

Kiersten tugged my arm towards the end of the hall, and opened the door.

We both froze.

She dropped my hand and covered her face.

White daffodils were spread across the bed in the shape of a heart. In the middle, our initials stood out against the red satin.

A small trail of orange and yellow daffodils led us to the bed and to a waiting desk with a bottle of champagne and a card.

Kiersten picked it up and nodded once, twice, then shook her head and handed it to me without saying anything.

Snatching it, I read the first few lines.

> *Wes Freaking Michels. HAH! Fun fact, Daffodils are symbolic of new beginnings and fresh starts. Thus, the reason your room is littered with them. Saylor never wants to see another daffodil in her entire life so please, keep all flowers contained lest she stuff one in my mouth while I'm sleeping. I love you two. I was trying to think of a wedding gift that would do you both justice—that would show my love for my best friends. All that kept*

coming to me was that you guys got a second chance to write a very original story. A love story. One that's so epic that even your grandchildren won't believe it. So here you go. Attached to this note is a pen. I wrote the first part, hope you don't mind. Enjoy your wedding night, enjoy the new beginning, and know...you're stuck with me forever. Tell Kiersten not to roll her eyes. It's rude.

Laughing, I grabbed the simple pen that was taped to the card and flipped it over to see what Gabe had written.

"Girl runs into boy..." I read aloud.

Kiersten looked down at the card and read the next part, "Girl feels up boy."

I chuckled while Kiersten crossed her arms and scowled.

"Boy chases girl."

"Girl—" Kiersten's voice was hoarse. "—decides she wants to be chased."

The next part was hard for me to read, I wasn't sure why.

Kiersten put her hand over mine and slowly spoke for me. "Boy gets very sick."

"Girl—" I held Kiersten tight. "—sticks by his side."

"Boy and girl..." Tears streamed down Kiersten's face, and she sniffed softly before she continued. "...fall asleep holding hands, and he tells her that even death couldn't keep him from a lifetime of her smiles."

A tear fell from my face onto Kiersten's head as I murmured, "Boy lives."

"Girl lives," she whispered.

"They lived," we said in unison...

The last line was a picture of us together with a giant heart drawn around it. Under the picture Gabe had written... *So LIVE.*

Chapter Twelve

Love is beautiful. A gift from God. I think it's sad, how easily we throw around the word without actually understanding the sacrifice behind its meaning. Love in its definition isn't about a strong feeling towards someone, but an action. If people truly understood what it was—our world would be changed. Love is sacrifice, it's holding someone's hand even though you know they can't feel it, like Gabe did with Kimmy. Love's watching someone lose all their hair, and still finding them to be the most beautiful person you've ever come across. Love is more action than feeling…Love, isn't just the way Wes looks at me, but the way he serves everyone around him as if he is nothing—and they are everything.—Mrs. Weston Michels

Kiersten

Wes placed the card back on the table, and his hands had a slight shake to them as he leaned his weight against the wood.

The room was silent, except for our breathing.

"You." Wes nodded without looking at me. "Are a gift."

It was one of those moments where I wasn't sure if he

wanted me to answer him, I wasn't sure if he needed me to or if he was going to say more. All I knew was that I already felt the need to cry and I had no idea why!

"Historically, gifts were brought to kings in order to honor them." Slowly, Wes moved away from the table and approached me, sinking to his knees on the floor. "People would travel all over the world, bringing their most prized possessions to place them at the feet of king they wanted to honor."

He gripped my hands, his blue eyes flashing with determination. "It's weird, wanting to honor the gift rather than the recipient. But here I am, on my knees, in front of the most beautiful gift I've ever received. If a king was placed behind you, if an entire monarchy was watching me fall to my knees, I'd still fall. I'd still lay down in front of the gift rather than the ruler, because the gift is that precious to me. More than gold, more than diamonds, more than the most expensive jewels in the world. You are more rare…" He cupped my face, brushing a kiss across my lips. "…than the rarest of jewels. I'd search the world for you. If I lost you, if you lost me, I'd never stop searching…for the gift, for you, not the King, because the treasure is you."

Tears streamed down my face. I couldn't think, I couldn't…. Did this happen to people? In real life? The most beautiful man I'd ever laid eyes on, one of the richest men in the world, an NFL player was on his knees in front of me telling me that I was the most precious thing in the world.

Every girl should be told her worth the way Wes was telling me of mine. In that instant, my heart soared and I experienced true security. All because he told me I was important, special…a treasure.

Sniffling, I joined him on the floor, moving closer until we were chest-to-chest, both of us on our knees. "Then you're my gift."

Wes's gaze never wavered from my face.

"If there was a king behind you, an emperor, a czar, I'd still honor the gift before I honored the recipient."

Wes's forehead touched mine.

I reached out and touched his skin. The shirt he'd been wearing was in pieces in the other room. "Should I honor the gift now?" I asked breathlessly.

Wes's brow furrowed as if he was confused. And then my hand moved to his belt, easily slipping it from his pants.

"Yeah." His smile was warm, inviting. "I think—" His voice cracked. "I would like that."

Wes's mouth was on mine, coaxing it open with his tongue before my hands were able to move any farther. My fingertips paused on his skin, feeling his warmth, memorizing the way his every exhale responded to my touch.

"Sweetheart…" he whispered, lips grazing mine over and over again like he was nibbling and tasting rather than kissing.

"Hmm…" My hands were seriously paralyzed, as if I wanted to peel back every layer of clothing separating us, but I could only focus on one thing at a time, and right now, he was tasting me and that was all I could think about. The way his tongue pressed against the inside of my mouth, the way he kissed, it was like he was trying to make love with his mouth—before anything else ever even happened. No wonder I had fallen hard and fast for the man—he was, incredible.

"I'm going to help you take off your dress." His mouth moved to my ear, kissing my neck and then returning to my ear to whisper, "And then…" his voice trailed off.

My heart pounded. And then? I waited, but Wes was already working with the zipper of my dress. In a swift movement, he had me pulled to my feet as my dress fell to the floor.

He stared at my silver stiletto heels and then slowly, his gaze rose from the heels to my knees, where he stopped again. I fought the urge to hide, his stare was so…hungry, so possessive. When his eyes reached the garters, he cursed softly, tore his gaze away, then cursed some more.

Wes reached out and pulled my hips towards him. "I have this really stupid, male desire to just…" He shook his head. "Damn, to just rip apart every stitch of clothing you have on. With my teeth. Then put it back on you, only so I can enjoy the feeling of my teeth grazing your skin as I rip those garters back off again. Over and over again. I doubt I'd tire of the process. Then again, it just prolongs the inevitable."

"The inevitable?" I pressed my body against his.

"Hell." He closed his eyes. "The inevitable, when I'm inside you."

Inside.

The word itself caused my entire body to flare to life. Adrenaline surged through my system. "So, what are you waiting for?"

Wes chuckled. "Oh, I'm not waiting, I'm…taking a time out."

"A time out?" I repeated. "Like in Football."

Wes licked his lips and winked. "The quarterback needs to tell the rest of the team the play."

"You're a one man team." I pointed out.

"Oh sweetheart…" He captured my mouth with his briefly then pulled back. "It's cute that you think that."

Before I had a chance to respond he lifted me into the air and carried me over to the bed, I had no choice but to wrap my legs around him and hold on as he softly joined me, his body hovering over mine.

"I'm not sure if I should be horrified that you think I'm a one-man team…" Wes slowly lowered his head to my thigh and winked. "Or amused."

My body arched as he bit the garter, his tongue dancing around the inside of my thigh as he explored every inch of territory, his teeth emerged, nibbling the same place he'd just kissed.

I let out a moan.

"Teeth, tongue…" Wes peered up at me and crooked his finger. "And imagine, that was just my mouth."

"Uhh—"

He silenced me by very slowly peeling down the stockings, throwing the garters behind him, and then tilting his head as he examined my lacy white underwear.

I shifted uncomfortably. It was nerve wracking having a man that beautiful stare at me like that.

"Remind me…" He leaned down, kissing the white lace at the top of the panties. "To buy out Victoria's Secret."

"Hilarious…" My raspy laugh turned into a gasp as he slowly peeled the panties down and continued kissing.

"Nothing funny about it." He blew across my skin. "I just want to see you in nothing but this for the rest of my life—that too much to ask?"

"N-no." His fingers grabbed the thin piece of material holding the underwear in place, and slowly slid them off. What I saw in Wes's eyes made my heart soar. It wasn't just approval, it was awe.

Chapter Thirteen

Every touch. Every caress. Every brush of skin against skin was like getting a shot of electricity directly into my heart. It was like being brought back to a world of light, after a lifetime of darkness. –Wes Michels

Wes

There were no words I could use to explain to Kiersten what I saw when I looked at her.

I'm sure they existed. I just didn't know them yet or hadn't been gifted with adequate logical thought to pull them out of the air and use them. I was too distracted by her red hair and green eyes, and the white garters that seriously almost stopped my heart all over again.

And then her tan skin against the white? It was too much. I actually wondered if it was possible for a man to have a stroke just because his sensory organs were taking in too much all at once.

Like being placed in front of a strobe light or something.

My eyes couldn't open wide enough.

My hands couldn't explore enough.

Damn, but God had had perfection in mind when he'd made this girl. She was….just…beautiful, effortlessly so.

From her high cheekbones to her mop of red hair spilling all over the white satin pillowcase.

I hadn't really had a lot of control to begin with. So I knew I was on borrowed time as she tilted my chin up and then leaned down to kiss me.

That one touch. That one innocent kiss. Was enough to set me on fire.

With a growl, I pushed her back onto the bed, pressing her body into the mattress, covering her with my own. With one hand I cupped her face while my other caressed her side.

Kiersten's hands moved to my pants. I lifted my body off her briefly so that I could slide them off.

But sliding hadn't been her plan. She broke off our kiss and with a jerk used both hands to tug my pants down. I didn't have time to stop her or tell her to go slower or try to be romantic—because her next action rendered me unconscious, or maybe just speechless?

Boxers? Gone.

Nothing.

But.

Skin.

If there was ever a time to cry tears of joy—now would be it. Kiersten wrapped her arms around my neck, and our bodies fit, so perfectly that it had to be a trick of the mind. How was that even possible?

I tried slowing down my kiss, the retreat was so hard it was painful, but Kiersten held onto my head so tight that I couldn't help but plunge my tongue into the depths of her mouth and lose myself.

Kiersten let out a tiny moan as my hands moved to brace her hips, and then I slid inside her, slowly at first, only because I knew if I went any faster, I would cease to make the night memorable for her.

Kiersten's hands dug into my back, causing me to arch up and take her with me... "Shit," I muttered through clenched teeth. The friction of the movement almost made me black out.

"Oh..." Kiersten's eyes fluttered open then closed. "Did I hurt you?"

"What?" I roared. "No, no, not hurting, definitely—" I stopped talking. What the hell was I doing? "Yeah, Kiersten, it hurts, right here." I kissed her softly and then pushed farther into her, then retreated. "Think you could help with that?"

She shrugged innocently, then locked her legs behind my back, pulling me all the way into her body—inviting me in, coaxing me, killing me.

Sweet death.

Everything about her was warm—tight—perfect. I gritted my teeth together.

"How's it feel now?" Her mouth met mine in a frenzied kiss.

"Like—" Control snapped. I pumped into her, taking her with me. "Perfection."

The buildup of what we had gone through over the last year...

Exploded into such an intense feeling of satisfaction, belonging, rightness, that when my body reached its tipping point, I physically shook as every muscle tightened and then released. Kiersten's soft cry washed over me as I carried her with me. Kiersten shuddered, waves of heat rolling off of her as I stayed put—never wanting to move from that position—ever.

Slowly, her green eyes opened, flashing with possession and a fierce type of love that made me want to cry. "I'm yours," Kiersten whispered, while I caught my breath. "And you are mine."

****

We stayed up all night.

And we weren't playing cards. Not unless cards was a new code word for sex, and the game was to see how many times we could actually participate in said activities until I died of dehydration and/or jumped into Elliot Bay.

At around seven in the morning the next day, I went to make a cup of coffee for Kiersten. At some point in the middle of the night her hair had become possessed with a rat and was now wrapped around her head like a really scary looking towel after Chewbacca had used it.

Once the coffee was brewed, I brought a mug to bed and watched her sleep. Rays morning sun peeked through the window. How had I been so blessed? To be gifted with not only life but with her? A year ago I should have died—instead I had a wife. I had Kiersten. I didn't want this moment to end, this morning. I wanted a thousand of them, a million, as many as my body could handle, that's how many I wanted. Sighing with contentment, I pulled up the blinds letting sunlight stream into the room.

"Why?" Kiersten grumbled from her bed. It was a true miracle her hair hadn't strangled her in her sleep. Her lips pressed together like she was trying not to smile.

"Why, what?" I set her mug on the bedside table.

"Why is there sun?"

Chuckling, I took a sip of coffee. "Oh you know, just this little thing called living...we need the sun in order to do it."

"You," Kiersten whispered. "I just need you." She pushed the mop of hair out of her face and rose from the bed, the sheet pooling at her hips. Without looking down, she grabbed her coffee and started drinking.

I, however, was still staring at her naked body.

Yeah, we'd been up all night, but I was ready to be up all morning too.

"So..." Kiersten continued talking as if she wasn't naked.

As if I had self control—which I totally didn't, not after I knew how good we were together. Not after the bathroom incident, where I'm pretty sure I made up new uses for soap, towels, and full length mirrors.

"What are doing today?"

"Damn it." Her breasts rose with each breath. How were they so pretty? Perky? The perfect size for my hands?

"We're cursing today?" Her brow furrowed.

"No." I shook my head, my throat was so damn dry you'd think I'd spent last night in the middle of the Sahara desert. "We're going to um..."

Kiersten leaned down and set her coffee back on the table.

Her breasts brushed my arm.

I clenched my teeth.

Gentle, Wes, be gentle.

Groaning, I pinched the bridge of my nose just as Kiersten peeked through her hair and gave me a coy look.

"Tease!" I yelled, setting my coffee next to hers. "Do you even, realize... and then words...not coming...but needing gentleness."

Kiersten burst out laughing. "Complete sentences."

Damn it!

"How do you know these things?" I shuddered as her hands gripped my ass hard, and then dipped into my boxers. Yeah, right there, shit..."I thought I was the teacher?"

Kiersten squeezed and giggled. "Lisa talked with me."

"Good because if it was Gabe talking to you about how to please me in bed I would have him by the balls, then again, I'd also be concerned he'd be into it since he'd know...you know what?" I cursed as Kiersten moved her hand. "Let's not talk."

Kiersten grabbed me by the back of the head and kissed me hard on the mouth then bit my lower lip, followed with smaller bites down my neck, when her tongue touched my nipple I almost fell backwards on my ass.

With a roar, I pounced onto the bed, threw off my boxers and t-shirt, and trapped her beneath my body. She was on her stomach laughing her ass off. And I was trying to think of ways I could both punish and please her at the same time.

My body...chose please.

"I love you," I whispered in her ear as my hands moved to her hips lifting her at the angle I needed.

"What are you do—" Kiersten sighed happily.

"Oh..." I chuckled and eased into her, immensely grateful that apparently Lisa hadn't told her everything. "The things I'll teach you."

"Yes, please." She moved against me.

With clenched teeth, I let out a hoarse cry. "Say please again, I really liked hearing that word from your lips."

"No." She gripped the pillow in front of her and panted. "Not a chance."

I pulled out of her. The emptiness was damn near devastating.

"But Wes—"

With a chuckle, I plunged into her and pulled her body tight against me. "Not really in a position to argue, are you sweetheart?"

"Please?"

"Please what?"

"Please...Wes?"

"That's my girl." Every angle felt different, every movement was pure torture and pleasure all wrapped up into one.

She never finished her coffee.

I never even made breakfast.

That was how we spent our morning.

We missed our flight to the Bahamas.

But I didn't care. There were always flights. But moments? Moments with a girl like that? I knew they were one in a million and I was on a mission to capture them all. Each. And every. One.

Chapter Fourteen

The thing about memories? They store in your brain. You can go a lifetime thinking you're totally fine and then boom, something triggers said memory and all of a sudden you're in the fetal position. My memory had always been really good—something I hated about myself because right now, I really, really wanted to have amnesia. —Lisa

Lisa

"You can't just tease and not follow through," Taylor said. "Besides, I'm just taking what everyone else has already had the chance to sample." His hands moved from my hips to my jeans, slowly undoing the zipper. "If you scream, I'll just be that much more entertained."

I woke up screaming.

And then, terrified that it was real and screaming would summon him, I slammed my hand over my mouth in order to muffle the sound of terror coming from my lips.

Reaching for my phone, I looked at the time—three am. I needed sleep if I had any hope of being awake for classes the next day. Today, I corrected myself.

With a grunt, I lay back down, and set my phone on the table. My hand brushed something. Curious, I turned on the light and looked down at the floor. It was an old picture of me.

Scrawled across the front at an angle were words that send a chill along my spine: *Taylor and Melanie Forever.*

Gagging, I barely made it to the bathroom before I lost all of my dinner from the night before.

With shaking hands, I looked at my reflection in the mirror. He couldn't' hurt me. He was gone. The picture was an old picture. It had probably found its way into my room from all the stacks of fan mail Gabe had been bringing in once he went to the media.

It was silly.

It meant nothing.

But the memory of his touch? I meant *some*thing, because with his touch he'd destroyed an innocence I would never get back. An innocence I'd fought for four years to forget about.

Because that's the thing about girls. We may talk a big game, we may say we're guys' equals. We may even say it's fine for us to sleep around. But the truth? I still wanted someone to want me. And I still wanted to be whole for them.

But I wasn't whole.

Because he'd stolen that piece of me—and I knew, even though he might be gone, I couldn't get those pieces back. They were lost forever.

My text alert went off.

Gabe: *You okay? Got up to get a drink of water and thought of you, you know you can stay with us this semester. No need for you to room alone. Oh and PS Wes and Kiersten made it safely into the Bahamas—two days late.*

Me: *It's fine. I think I may live off campus this year. I'll figure it out. No worries! Gotta sleep. Yay for the happy couple!*

I sighed and threw the phone onto my bed, chewing my lower lip in the process. Everyone was moving on with their lives.

And I was stuck.

Rain pelted my window. Funny, because I felt like rain most the time. Like I was meant to be sunshine but got confused and haven't been able to free myself of the darkness for a really long time.

With a pitiful sigh, I crawled back into bed and closed my eyes. I prayed he wouldn't visit me in my dreams again. Because whenever he visited—I was reminded of how pathetic it really was.

To want a love like Wes and Kiersten or Gabe and Saylor. To think it actually accessible, when all signs pointed to the obvious.

It would never happen. Not to me.

My heart broke all over again as warm tears slid off my cheeks onto the pillows. It wouldn't happen for me, but I could still be the best person I could be, right? Right. That had to be enough.

Want more of the Ruin series?

Check out the next book in the series, *Shame*, Lisa's story, with special appearances from the rest of the gang we've all grown to love so much. ;)

About the Author

Rachel Van Dyken is the *New York Times, Wall Street Journal,* and *USA Today* bestselling author of regency and contemporary romances. When she's not writing you can find her drinking coffee at Starbucks and plotting her next book while watching *The Bachelor.*

She keeps her home in Idaho with her husband and their snoring boxer, Sir Winston Churchill. She loves to hear from readers! You can follow her writing journey at www.rachelvandykenauthor.com

Other Books by Rachel Van Dyken

Forever Romance
The Bet
The Wager
Elite
Elect

Seaside Series
Tear
Pull
Shatter
Forever
Fall

Wallflower Trilogy
Waltzing with the Wallflower
Beguiling Bridget
Taming Wilde

London Fairy Tales
Upon a Midnight Dream
Whispered Music
The Wolf's Pursuit

Renwick House
The Ugly Duckling Debutante
The Seduction of Sebastian St. James
The Redemption of Lord Rawlings
An Unlikely Alliance
The Devil Duke Takes a Bride

Other Titles
Every Girl Does It
The Parting Gift

Compromising Kessen
Savage Winter
Divine Uprising
Ruin
Toxic

www.rachelvandykenauthor.com
Twitter: @RachVD
Facebook: RachelVanDyken

Made in the USA
Columbia, SC
03 October 2017